CAUGHT IN SMILES

ISBN# 1-930710-49-6
Copyright ©2000 Veritas Press

All rights reserved. No part of this book may be reproduced or transmitted in any form or by any means, electronic or mechanical, including photocopying, recording, or by any information storage and retrieval system, without permission in writing from the publisher.

Veritas Press, Lancaster, Pennsylvania
800-922-5082
www.VeritasPress.com

First edition

CAUGHT IN SMILES

STORY BY
DOUGLAS
JONES

IMAGES BY
PAULA
MARSTON

Veritas Press

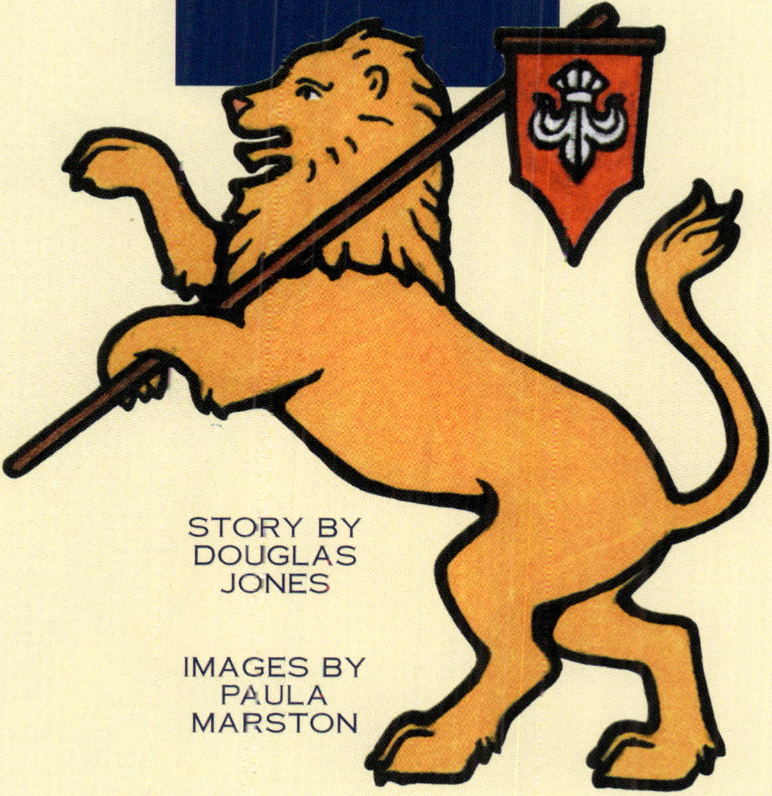

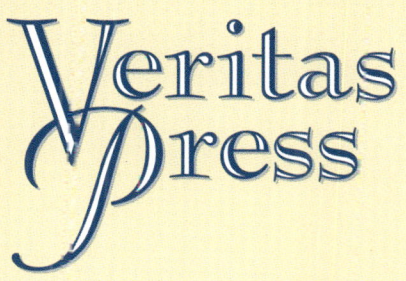

The Queen Mother of France threw the vase at the wall, and it broke into a spray of green pieces. Her helpers ran from her room, and she shouted them back.

They came back and stood there shaking and staring down. The Queen Mother, Catherine, shook her head but then started to smile slowly.

"If I can not frighten Henry with wrath, then I will spoil him with fun," she said. "Go. Bring Henry here for a celebration. And do not let his mother know."

Henry was less than thirteen, but he had been brought to Paris by his wretch of a father to study. Henry was in line to be king. His mother Jeanne was a godly Christian queen

of a small land in the south of France. Catherine longed to turn Henry from his mother's ways to her twisted path.

When at last Henry came to Catherine, she played the part of a fawning and beaming grandmother, loading him with gifts of toys and games and sweets of all kinds.

She gave him armor and swords and horses to ride and boats to sail.

He had the best robes and a big room, all plush and full of flaunting things. She brought him boys to sport with and race, but they had to let Henry win at games.

She brought him coy, blushing girls to praise his jokes, call him cute, and kiss his cheek. He did not have to clean up his messes or eat all of his feast or go to bed.

Catherine made sure that no one would say "no" to him or chide his bad actions. By this, Catherine hoped to train Henry to be weak

and foolish so when he was king she could rule him. She liked the work of her hands.

Catherine then brought Henry into her meetings and played as if Henry was a wise man and asked his thoughts on big plans. At that time, Catherine and her men were

thinking of ways to get rid of all those in France who loved God's grace and hated the idols that Catherine loved. They talked of killing them.

Henry's face was strong, but he knew their plans would harm his mother Jeanne. Jeanne knew that Catherine hated her and her godly life. Yet Catherine thought she could win

Jeanne too by raining phony love on her. At last, Catherine came from afar and brought Henry with her to visit his mother.

Catherine hugged and kissed Jeanne and poured fine gifts on her. Yet Jeanne could see how Henry was changed.

Catherine took Henry back to Paris, but Jeanne was sick with fear for her son. Jeanne knew she had to free Henry from Catherine, but Catherine was so strong.

After much praying, Jeanne called a small band of her men and left for Paris. Catherine was all smiles, when they came to her. She brought them in and held feasts and celebrations for them for days. Jeanne and

her men longed to take Henry and leave. But when they tried to leave, Catherine would make up a new feast or call a dance or bring new visitors she said they just had to meet.

Catherine did not lock them in, but she made it rude for them to leave. They were trapped. After weeks there, Jeanne started looking for tricky ways to leave. One day she found one. Catherine had called for a sporting

hunt out in her lands. Jeanne and her men went, too. Before they all left, she made a plan with Henry and her men to meet at a place in the fields.

Before that, Jeanne had left a note for Catherine to find later. As the hunt went on, the time came to meet out on the far fields. Jeanne, Henry, and her men played as if they got lost from the hunt. They were soon so far

that Catherine could not see them, and Henry was willing to go. They turned their horses south to Jeanne's land and took flight for days and days.

When Catherine later found Jeanne's note, Jeanne had said that she was thankful for all the good from Catherine, but it would be too sad to say farewell face to face. Catherine was steaming. Back in their own land, Henry

loved his mother, and Jeanne did her best to train Henry with good and godly men.

Yet Catherine's spoiling would be hard to turn back. Later he did rise to be king of France.